THE *Princess* IN *BLACK*
and the *BATHTIME BATTLE*

THE *Princess* IN BLACK
and the BATHTIME BATTLE

Shannon Hale & Dean Hale

illustrated by
LeUyen Pham

CANDLEWICK PRESS

Text copyright © 2019 by Shannon and Dean Hale
Illustrations copyright © 2019 by LeUyen Pham

First edition 2019

Library of Congress Catalog Card Number 2019939807
ISBN 978-1-5362-0221-2

19 20 21 22 23 24 LEO 10 9 8 7 6 5 4 3 2 1

Printed in Heshan, Guangdong, China

This book was typeset in LTC Kennerley Pro.
The illustrations were done in watercolor and ink.

Candlewick Press
99 Dover Street
Somerville, Massachusetts 02144

visit us at www.candlewick.com

*For Addie, and
for her mom, Deb,
who got the band together*

S. H., D. H.,
and L. P.

Chapter 1

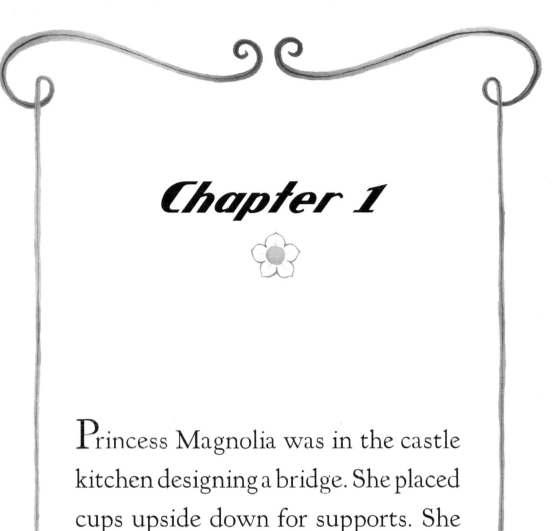

Princess Magnolia was in the castle kitchen designing a bridge. She placed cups upside down for supports. She balanced spoons and forks on top. She held her breath. But they all tumbled down.

Too many forks and not enough supports. She would have to start over.

"Well, that stinks," said Princess Magnolia.

Just then, an alarming smell floated through the window. Princess Magnolia stuck out her tongue.

"No," she said, "*that* stinks."

She checked her glitter-stone ring. It wasn't ringing. No monster alarm. Just an alarming smell. This smelled like a problem for the Princess in Black.

A few minutes later, the Princess in Black and Blacky were galloping away from the castle.

"Do you smell it too, Blacky?" she asked.

Blacky sneezed. He most definitely smelled it. And he'd prefer to never smell it again.

They followed the odor all the way to the goat pasture. The goats were gagging. The goats were gasping. A squirrel was turning green.

"I'm glad you've come," said the Goat Avenger. "We've got trouble."

"It sure smells like trouble," said the Princess in Black.

The Goat Avenger kicked the cloud of stench. "We can't battle it, Princess in Black."

She punched the cloud of stink. "Our ninja moves do nothing, Goat Avenger."

"Yah!" the Goat Avenger shouted.
He kicked the stink harder. His foot
passed through it. He fell on his bum.

Blacky neighed. He swished his tail.

"Great idea, Blacky!" said the Princess in Black.

She opened her fan. She fanned her fan at the smell.

"It's working!" said the Goat Avenger.

The stench floated away to the south. At last the pasture air was stink-free. The goats cheered. The Princess in Black and the Goat Avenger had saved the day!

Chapter 2

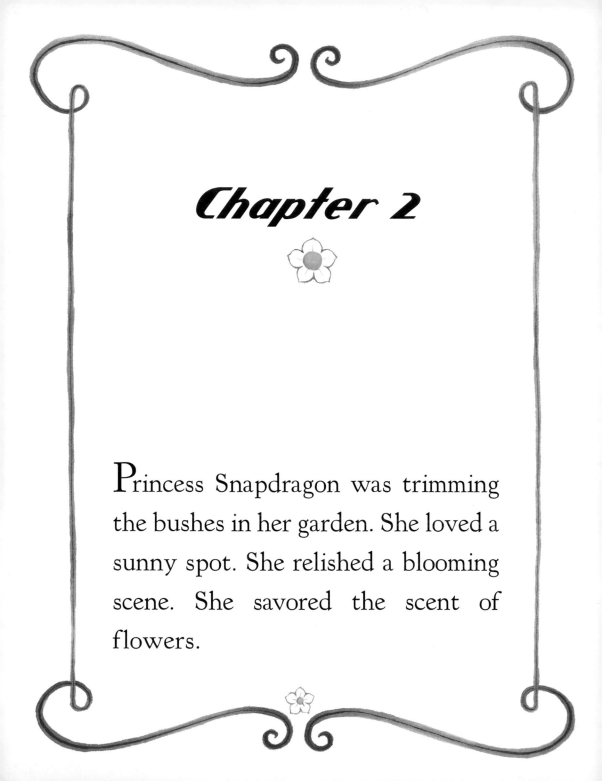

Princess Snapdragon was trimming the bushes in her garden. She loved a sunny spot. She relished a blooming scene. She savored the scent of flowers.

Suddenly, a stink blew into the garden. The roses sagged, and the lilies curled up. The bluebells turned green.

Her pet dragon, Moonwhistle, crouched behind the buttercups. She covered her snout.

"Oh, Moonwhistle," said Princess Snapdragon. "This odor is alarming. I wish I could make it go away."

Moonwhistle hopped up. She pointed a wing at the garden shed, where they kept their secret disguises.

"You're right, Moonwhistle," said Princess Snapdragon. "We've prepared for this day! It's time at last!"

Together they flew into the shed. When they flew out, they were no longer Princess Snapdragon and Moonwhistle the dragon.

They followed the stench out of their kingdom. They followed the stink right into the goat pasture.

"Wow!" said the Goat Avenger. "Another masked hero!"

"It is I, Flower Girl!" said Flower Girl. She tossed a handful of rose petals. It was a nice touch. "And this is my faithful companion, Horsefly the pegasus."

"Always nice . . . to meet . . . another hero!" said the Princess in Black. She was out of breath from all the fanning.

"Um, Princess in Black?" said Flower Girl. "You are fanning that horrible smell to the south. And to the south is Princess Snapdragon's kingdom."

"Oh, no! That stinks!" said the Princess in Black.

"It certainly does," said the Goat Avenger, wrinkling his nose.

"Perhaps we can chase the smell away . . . with flowers!" said Flower Girl.

Horsefly landed on the grass, and Flower Girl handed out bouquets of roses. The heroes and animals batted their bouquets at the stink. It slithered away to the west.

Now the day was saved, thanks to the three heroes and their faithful companions!

Chapter 3

Princess Honeysuckle was dancing in her courtyard. She loved a flying leap. She relished a low crouch. She savored the joy of the dance.

Suddenly she heard cries of alarm.

"Fur Suit, what's happening?" she asked her pet wolf.

Fur Suit whined.

In the courtyard trees, the songbirds were gasping. The songbirds were gagging. A bluebird turned green.

"What a horrible stench!" said Princess Honeysuckle. "Fur Suit, I think it might be time."

Fur Suit smiled a wolf smile.

The princess and wolf sneaked into the gazebo. They put on disguises. Then they rode straight to the goat pasture.

"It is I, Cartwheel Queen!" Cartwheel Queen did a cartwheel. It was a very good cartwheel. "And this isn't a wolf. This is my dog. His name is Good Boy."

Good Boy barked. It was a pretty good bark.

"Always nice to meet a new hero!" said the Princess in Black.

"We followed a terrible odor all the way from Princess Honeysuckle's kingdom in the west," said Cartwheel Queen. "Do you know where it's coming from?"

The three heroes smiled sheepishly. The goats smiled goatishly.

"We must have sent it there," said Flower Girl.

"Hmm, how to get rid of this smell?" asked Cartwheel Queen. She did another cartwheel. Cartwheels helped her to think.

"Your cartwheel gave me an idea!" said the Goat Avenger.

Cartwheel Queen helped him fetch the goats' summer fan. They set it by the hole to Monster Land and pointed it up. The fan's blades spun as fast as a cartwheel. The wind from the fan pushed the stink into the clouds.

And now, at last, the day was saved, thanks to four brave heroes and their fearless companions!

Chapter 4

Princess Orchid was trying out the new zip line she'd built in the village playground. She loved a good whoosh. She relished a thrilling ride. She savored the swooshing of the wind.

But then she zip-lined right through a cloud of stink.

"Ugh!" said Princess Orchid, falling down.

All around her, children were gagging. Children were gasping. One boy turned green. It was the smelliest smell anyone had ever smelled.

"Help!" said a little girl. "It's so gross!"

"The smell . . ." said a little boy, falling to his knees. "THE SMELL!"

"I'll fix this," said Princess Orchid. "Somehow."

Princess Orchid zip-lined back to her castle.

"Nottamoose!" Princess Orchid called out to her reindeer. Who was not a moose.

Nottamoose followed her into the workshop. Princess Orchid whispered into her fur-tipped ear. "The time has come."

Nottamoose nodded. She slipped socks shaped like bunny ears over her antlers.

They spotted the stinky trail going up into the clouds. It came down again at the goat pasture. Where a whole bunch of heroes were standing around a hole and a fan.

"It is I, Miss Fix-It!" said Miss Fix-It. "And this is my faithful companion, Doom Rabbit the bunny."

Doom Rabbit nodded. Her sock
ears flopped up and down.

"I guess you've come from the
north?" said Cartwheel Queen.

"Where there was a horrible smell?" said the Goat Avenger.

"And you've come to stop it?" said the Princess in Black.

"Yes, exactly," said Miss Fix-It.

"We tried to push the stink up," said Flower Girl.

"What goes up must come down," said Miss Fix-It. "And it came down into my — uh, into Princess Orchid's kingdom."

The Goat Avenger turned off the fan. And the stink once again settled on the goat pasture. The goats whimpered. One fell over with its hooves in the air.

"If it were a monster, I'd know what to do," said the Princess in Black. "But how do you fight a stink?"

Chapter 5

Down in Monster Land, the monsters were groaning. The monsters were griping. A blue monster turned turquoise. All because of one extremely stinky monster.

Usually monsters enjoyed a good stink. They liked the moldy, dark corners of caves. They enjoyed rotten fruit. Above all, they adored the odor of goats.

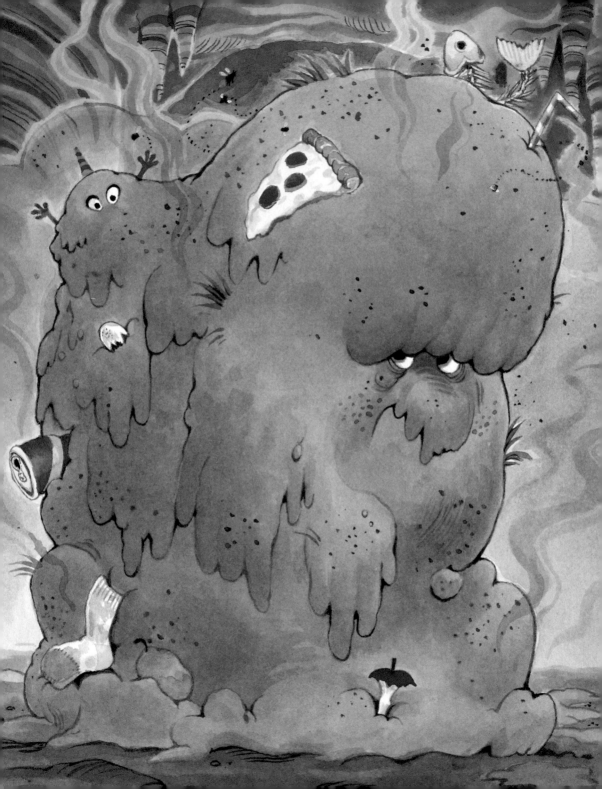

But the stinky monster was too much. Rotten fruit smooshed between its toes. Garbage clung to its back. Who knew what that stuff was on its head? There was even a tiny monster tangled in its filthy fur. It'd been stuck there since last week.

Two big-nosed monsters could not stand it anymore. They plugged their faces. They grabbed the stinky monster. And they jumped up right out of Monster Land.

The big-nosed monsters dropped
the stinky monster in the goat pasture.
They wiped their paws on the grass,
and they didn't even try to eat goats.

They just jumped back into Monster
Land as fast as they could go, away
from that stinky monster.

Chapter 6

The heroes struck battle poses. The stink was a monster after all! And there it sat. In the goat pasture. Being stinky.

The stinky monster chewed on a dirty claw. It waved.

"At last, we can fight the stink!" said the Princess in Black. "As soon as that monster says EAT GOATS, let's wage battle."

"EEEURP," the stinky monster burped.

The Goat Avenger said, "You may not eat the —"

"Wait," said the Princess in Black. "It didn't say EAT GOATS yet. That was just a burp."

Cartwheel Queen plugged her nose. "A stinky burp," she said.

"Back, burp!" Flower Girl shouted. She fanned her bouquet at the burp.

"Yes, let's try some battle cries," said the Princess in Black. "Behave, beast!"

The stinky monster wiped its nose on the back of its paw.

"Back! Back to your infernal pit!" said the Goat Avenger.

The stinky monster scratched under its armpit. A goat gagged.

"You may not gag the goats!" shouted Miss Fix-It.

The stinky monster lay down on its back. It watched the clouds float by.

"Um . . . monster?" said the Princess in Black.

The stinky monster plucked goo from its ear. It brushed the goo through its head fur.

"How do we fix this?" asked Miss Fix-It.

Chapter 7

The Princess in Blankets and her unicorn, Corny, trotted into the goat pasture. She had come for a hero princess playdate. The pasture was the perfect place for a playdate. Sunshine! Grassy slopes! Fresh air!

And sometimes monsters came out
of the hole so they could wage battle.

Hooray! There was a monster in
the pasture today. And more friends!
She waved.

"The princess is blanketed!" she started to shout. But then the stink cloud hit her.

"Urk!" she said, toppling off Corny's back. "What happened . . . to all the fresh air?"

Washcloths spilled off her hat.
Miss Fix-It picked them up.

"Hmm," said Miss Fix-It. "What
if we —"

"Give the monster a bath!" the hero princesses all said together.

The Goat Avenger would have said it too, but he was running to the shed to fetch the goats' tub.

Chapter 8

The stinky monster was stinkier than a full litter box. It was stinkier than a clogged toilet. It was stinkier than a pile of dirty diapers on a hot summer day.

The stinky monster was so stinky, it was more stink than monster.

The heroes were armed with washcloths and scrub brushes. Water buckets and goat soap. And one big, goat-sized tub. But the stink was too gross.

"The stink . . . it's . . . too gross," said the Princess in Blankets.

They couldn't get near the monster.

"We can't even get near the monster!" said Flower Girl.

The Princess in Black pointed at the tub.

"Monster, you need a bath," she said.

"NO," said the monster. "NO BATH."

"Behave, beast!" said Cartwheel Queen. "And get in the tub!"

"NO BATH!" said the monster.
"Udders and moo cows!" said the
Princess in Blankets. "What can we do?"

Chapter 9

The Goat Avenger took a deep breath and then ran into the stink cloud. He said, "AAAAH!" Then he said, "Ugh. . . ." And then he fainted from the smell.

The Princess in Black hooked the Goat Avenger's ankle with a rope. She pulled him back to safety.

"Heroes," she said, "none of us can do this alone. We need support. We need to work together."

"Hmm, we can't get near it," said Miss Fix-It. "So maybe we can wash it from a distance."

"A big distance," said Flower Girl.

So they made a plan. From a big distance.

"Ready?" said Miss Fix-It.

Flower Girl leaped onto Horsefly's back. Cartwheel Queen put her hands up, ready to cartwheel. The Princess in Black and the Princess in Blankets aimed hoses.

"Now!" said Miss Fix-It.

The Goat Avenger turned on the water. Cartwheel Queen cartwheeled around the monster, spraying soap as she went. From above, Flower Girl dropped bath bombs.

The monster roared. It was a huge, bubbly, soaking-wet mess. The stink wasn't gone, but it was better than before. Now the heroes could get closer.

"NO BATH!" roared the monster.

"Yes bath!" said the Princess in Black.

"EAT BATH!" roared the monster. It swallowed the water. And some of the soap. It took a bite out of the tub. And it burped up a bath bomb.

"You may not eat your bath!" said the Princess in Black.

And so the heroes and the stinky monster waged bathtime.

Chapter 10

The heroes didn't stop until there was no more stinky monster. Now it was a fluffy monster. It was the fluffiest fluff of a monster the heroes had ever seen.

"Aww, it's so cute!" said Flower Girl.

The fluffy monster sniffed its fur.
It snuffled its armpits. It sighed a
sigh of relief.

So did the tiny monster, finally
untangled from the funky fur.

"Aww, they're the cutest!" said Flower Girl.

The monsters sniffed the air. Now that the stink was gone, they could smell the goats.

"GOATS!" said the tiny monster.

"EAT GOATS!" said the fluffy monster.

The heroes struck battle poses.

"You may not eat the goats!" they got to say at last.

There were a lot of heroes. The monsters looked at each other. They shrugged.

"OK," said the tiny monster.

"BYE-BYE," said the fluffy monster.

And together, they jumped back into Monster Land.

"Whew!" said the Princess in Black. "I never could have washed that stinky monster all by myself."

"That was a situation too stinky for a single hero," said the Goat Avenger.

"Yes, it's good to have support," said the Princess in Blankets. "How can we find you all if we need big help again?"

"I have an idea!" said Miss Fix-It. She showed them a small pink stone. "I discovered that when I shine a light through it, a pink sparkle twinkles up in the sky."

"I have a stone just like that!" said the Princess in Blankets. "Uh . . . Princess Sneezewort gave it to me."

"I got one from Princess Honeysuckle," said Cartwheel Queen.

"Mine was a gift from Princess Orchid!" said Miss Fix-It.

"And I have one from Princess Snapdragon," said Flower Girl.

"Isn't it wonderful," said the Princess in Black, "how many princesses and heroes are friends?"

"All of my friends are princesses and heroes," said the Goat Avenger. "Also goats. And a really interesting squirrel."

"Squeak," said the squirrel.

"Whenever we need help," said the Princess in Black, "we can shine a light into a stone. And the Sparkle Signal will show up in the sky."

"Who knows?" said the Princess in Blankets. "Maybe there are even more heroes out there. Maybe they'll see it too."